For my Grandkids
and to all my family and friends.
Thank you.
Not forgetting Lockdown for focusing the stories I've had in my head ior you.
Helen Watson.

First published in 2020 by Amazon.
Text copyright Helen Watson 2020.
Illustrations copyright Helen Watson 2020.

All rights reserved.
Imagination shared.

You thought you knew about Oor Haggis !

Well read again…..

and have fun colouring in too.

OOR HAGGIS

A wee look at the life and tales of Oor Haggis. The Wee Scottish Beastie.

OOR HAGGIS

Oor Haggis ,is a small furry little creature native to the Scottish hills above distilleries.

They have four legs. It was previously believed that two of their legs are shorter on one side or the other depending on whether they are left or right footed. Making it easier to run around the side of hills. This would only work in one direction. They have in fact shorter legs at the front and longer legs at the back. This helps with jumping and makes them faster at running.

Oor Haggis has fur similar to a cat's, but waterproof , windproof and most definitely warm. They grow an extra thick coat for winter & shed it in spring and summer.
Depending on which Clan they come from , varies the colour of their coats.
Highland Haggis are usually Black. Black helps them absorb heat from the sun. Central Scotland Haggis tend to be Dark Brown & Southern Scottish Haggis are either Brindle or Ginger in colour.

The female Haggis is called a Keilder or Hen and the male are called a Jock. The Keilder/Hen mates with four to six Jock's and can produce a brood of up to 8 Bairns, up to four times a year. The Bairn's stay with the Keilder/Hen for up to two years. She teaches them how to find food, run & jump. The Jock's supply the food and bedding. Once they are two years old , they leave the burrow to find their own mate. This is when they are introduced to drinking whisky.

A Big party is held to celebrate them leaving Hame.

The adults celebrate by drinking whisky & mating to make the next brood. The hills can get quite noisy at these times of the year as it usually coincides with the equinoxes .

Haggis eat heather and midges. They can jump up to four feet to catch midges. Usually off the top of rocks. Some have been found to eat daisies , buttercups and thistles. Even Haggis can become vegetarians when there's no midges about.

Haggis live in underground burrows on hills near distilleries. They look a bit like rabbit burrows, the only difference is the small whisky bottles lying around the entrance. The local councils are still in talks about trying to train them to use bottle banks. But SPCA don't want them trained by humans. It could affect the taste of the meat & the whisky industry don't want the extra cost of training and supplying the modified bottle banks.

The Haggis and the whisky distilleries have been working together , hand in hand for centuries.
The distilleries get the water to make their whisky from the hills and streams that the Haggis live on. If they set up on the wrong site , they don't get the full flavour or colour to their whisky. The distilleries would have you believe it's the wooden casks that do this. As that is what they do in other countries to get the colour and flavour. This is why Scottish Whisky is the best in the world. As nature intended.

Haggis have also been known to help shepherds get to sleep. Ever wondered where "counting sheep helps you sleep", comes from ? Haggis jump on the backs of the sheep and ride them past the shepherd while humming. This sends the shepherd off to sleep. It is also good for teaching the Bairn's balance and introduce them to humans before they leave the burrow.

To those who want to befriend a Haggis. You'll need a good singing voice, a handful of midges and some whisky. They are curious creatures, but wary of humans.

Sit quietly at night on the hillside under a full moon at midnight singing Scottish love songs. After three nights, they will know whether to trust you or not and can smell intention off you. They also get the Faerie Folk to check you out too. If they trust you , they will sing back to you. If they don't trust you , you might get a nasty bite on your ankle and make a noise a bit like an Adder.(snake)

But beware. It is against the   law to capture and keep a wild Haggis as a pet or even a zoo.

They would wreck your Hame and burst your eardrums with their squawking. They would signal for all the near hand wildlife to help rescue them. As they can't stand the noise either... So take heid.

Some have said local Faerie Folk would rescue them and put a curse on those who have tried. To always hear their squawking till they turn mad and can only eat porridge.

To catch a Haggis you must have patience, as it can take up to five days. First you must be able to find their burrows. Gamekeepers and Distillery owners usually know where they are.

You need a half bottle of whisky per burrow, a glass, a piece of string and some razor blades. On the first night , you put a glass of whisky at the opening of the burrow. They come out, look both ways to see if anyone is about. Then they drink the whisky. The second night , you put the whisky a few inches away from the burrow. They come out, look both ways and then drink the whisky. On the third night , you dip the string into the whisky. They can smell it. Tie the razor blades to the string and put it against the opening of the burrow. They only get to look one way.

Now animal rights protesters have been campaigning to have this method abolished for a more humane way. But are having to design a sound proof box in which to capture them. Or you would only be able to catch one per hillside per night. As they can squawk like a hawk and warn all the other Haggis burrows for miles around.

So next Burn's night, please remember Oor Haggis.

In tales of olde, it has been said that Rabbie Burns himself, sang to a Haggis Keilder/Hen elder and she inspired him to write "Ta A Haggis" in her honor. He was struck by her beauty and expresive eyes while sitt by the banks of Afton water.

Made in the USA
Monee, IL
24 November 2020

49379240R00015